# INSIDE EARTH

# INSIDE EARTH

by Poul Anderson

# I

The biotechnicians had been very thorough. I was already a little undersized, which meant that my height and build were suitable—I could pass for a big Earthling. And of course my face and hands and so on were all right, the Earthlings being a remarkably humanoid race. But the technicians had had to remodel my ears, blunting the tips and grafting on lobes and cutting the muscles that move them. My crest had to go and a scalp covered with revolting hair was now on the top of my skull.

Finally, and most difficult, there had been the matter of skin color. It just wasn't possible to eliminate my natural coppery pigmentation. So they had injected a substance akin to melanin, together with a virus which would manufacture it in my body, the result being a leathery brown. I could pass for a member of the so-called "white" subspecies, one who had spent most of his life in the open.

The mimicry was perfect. I hardly recognized the creature that looked out of the mirror. My lean, square, blunt-nosed face, gray eyes, and big hands were the same or nearly so. But my black crest had been replaced with a shock of blond hair, my ears were small and immobile, my skin a dull bronze, and several of Earth's languages were hypnotically implanted in my brain—together with a set of habits and reflexes making up a pseudo-personality which should be immune to any tests that the rebels could think of.

I *was* Earthling! And the disguise was self-perpetuating: the hair grew and the skin color was kept permanent by the artificial "disease." The biotechnicians had told me that if I kept the disguise long enough, till I began to age—say, in a century or so—the hair would actually thin and turn white as it did with the natives.

It was reassuring to think that once my job was over, I could be restored to normal. It would need another series of operations and as much time as the original transformation, but it would be as complete and scarless. I'd be human again.

# INSIDE EARTH

I put on the clothes they had furnished me, typical Earthly garments—rough trousers and shirt of bleached plant fibers, jacket and heavy shoes of animal skin, a battered old hat of matted fur known as felt. There were objects in my pockets, the usual money and papers, a claspknife, the pipe and tobacco I had trained myself to smoke and even to like. It all fitted into my character of a wandering, outdoors sort of man, an educated atavist.

I went out of the hospital with the long swinging stride of one accustomed to walking great distances.

*

The Center was busy around me. Behind me, the hospital and laboratories occupied a fairly small building, some eighty stories of stone and steel and plastic. On either side loomed the great warehouses, military barracks, officers' apartments, civilian concessions, filled with the vigorous life of the starways. Behind the monstrous wall, a mile to my right, was the spaceport, and I knew that a troopship had just lately dropped gravs from Valgolia herself.

The Center swarmed with young recruits off duty, gaping at the sights, swaggering in their new uniforms. Their skins shone like polished copper in the blistering sunlight, and their crests were beginning to wilt a little. All Earth is not the tropical jungle most Valgolians think it is—northern Europe is very pleasant, and Greenland is even a little on the cold side—but it gets hot enough at North America Center in midsummer to fry a shilast.

A cosmopolitan throng filled the walkways. Soldiers predominated—huge, shy Dacors, little slant-eyed Yangtusans, brawling Gorrads, all the manhood of Valgolia. Then there were other races, blue-skinned Vegans, furry Proximans, completely non-humanoid Sirians and Antarians. They were here as traders, observers, tourists, whatever else of a non-military nature one can imagine.

I made an absent-minded way through the crowds. A sudden crack on the side of my head, nearly bowling me over, brought me to awareness. I looked up into the arrogant face of one of the new recruits and heard him rasp, "Watch where you're going, Terrie!"

The young blood in the Valgolian military is deliberately trained to harshness, even brutality, for our militarism must impress such backward colonies as Earth. It goes against our grain, but it is necessary. At another time this might have annoyed me. I could have pulled rank on him. Not only was I an officer, but such treatment must be used with intellectual deliberation. The occasional young garrison trooper who comes here with the idea that the natives are an inferior breed to be kicked around misses the whole point of Empire. If, indeed, Earth's millions were an inferior breed, I wouldn't have been here at all. Valgol needs an economic empire, but if all we had in mind was serfdom we'd be perfectly content with the plodding animal life of Deneb VII or a hundred other worlds.

I cringed appropriately, as if I didn't understand Valgolian Universal, and slunk past him. But it griped me to be taken for a Terrie. If I was to become an Earthling, I would at least be a self-respecting one.

*

There were plenty of Terries—Terrestrials—around, of course, moving with their odd combination of slavish deference toward Valgolians and arrogant superiority toward mere Earthlings. They have adopted the habits and customs of civilization, entered the Imperial service, speak Valgolian even with their families. Many of them shave their heads save for a scalp lock, in imitation of the crest, and wear white robes suggesting those of civil functionaries at home.

I've always felt a little sorry for the class. They work, and study, and toady to us, and try so hard to be like us. It's frustrating, because that's exactly what we don't want. Valgolians are Valgolians and Earthlings are men of Earth. Well, Terries are important to the ultimate aims of the Empire, but not in the way they think they are. They serve as another symbol of Valgolian conquest for Earth to hate.

I entered the Administration Building. They expected me there and took me at once to the office of General Vorka, who's a general only as far as this solar system is concerned. Had there been any Earthlings around, I would have saluted to conform to the show of militarism, but General Vorka sat alone behind his desk, and I merely said, "Hello, Coordinator."

The sleeves of his tunic rolled up, the heat of North America beading his forehead with sweat, the big man looked up at me. "Ah, yes. I'm glad you're finally prepared. The sooner we get this thing started—" He extended a silver galla-dust box. "Sniff? Have a seat, Conru."

I inhaled gratefully and relaxed. The Coordinator picked up a sheaf of papers on his desk and leafed through them. "Umm-mm, only fifty-two years old and a captain already. Remarkably able, a young man like you. And your work hitherto has been outstanding. That Vegan business...."

I said yes, I knew, but could he please get down to business. You couldn't blame me for being a bit anxious to begin. Disguised as I was as an Earthman, I felt uncomfortable, embarrassed, almost, at being with my ex-countrymen.

The Coordinator shrugged. "Well, if you can carry this business off—fine. If you fail, you may die quite unpleasantly. That's their trouble, Conru: you wouldn't be regarded as an individual, but as a Valgolian. Did you know that they even make such distinctions among themselves? I mean races and sub-races and social castes and the like; it's keeping them divided and impotent, Conru. It's also keeping them out of the Empire. A shame."

*

I knew all that, of course, but I merely nodded. Coordinator Vorka was a wonderful man in his field, and if he tended to be on the garrulous side, what could I do? I said, "I know that, sir. I also know I was picked for a dangerous job because you thought I could fill the role. But I still don't know exactly what the job is."

8

Coordinator Vorka smiled. "I'm afraid I can't tell you much more than you must already have guessed," he said. "The anarch movement here—the rebels, that is—is getting no place, primarily because of internal difficulties. When members of the same group spit epithets at each other referring to what they consider racial or national distinctions which determine superiority or inferiority, the group is bound to be an insecure one. Such insecurity just does not make for a strong rebellion, Conru. They try, and we goad them—but dissention splits them constantly and their revolutions fizzle out.

"They just can't unite against us, can't unite at all. Conru, you know how we've tried to educate them. It's worked, too, to some extent. But you can't educate three billion people who have a whole cultural pattern behind them."

I winced. "Three billion?"

"Certainly. Earth is a rich planet, Conru, and a fairly crowded one at the same time. Bickering is inevitable. It's a part of their culture, as much as cooperation has been a part of ours."

I nodded. "We learned the hard way. The old Valgol was a poor planet and we had to unite to conquer space or we could not have survived."

The Coordinator sniffed again at his silver box. "Of course. And we're trying to help these people unite. They don't have to make the same mistakes we did, long ago. They don't have to at all. Get them to hate us enough, get them to hate us until all their own clannish hatreds don't count at all.... Well, you know what happened on Samtrak."

I knew. The Samtraks are now the entrepreneurs of the Empire, really ingenious traders, but within the memory of some of our older men they were a sore-spot. They didn't understand the meaning of Empire any more than Earth does, and they never did understand it until we goaded them into open rebellion. The very reverse of divide and rule, you might say, and it worked. We withdrew trading privileges one by one, until they revolted successfully, thus educating themselves sociologically in only a few generations.

*

Vorka said, "The problem of Earth is not quite that simple." He leaned back, made a bridge of his fingers, and peered across them at me. "Do you know precisely what a provocateur job is, Conru?"

I said that I did, but only in a hazy way, because until now my work had been pretty much restricted to social relations on the more advanced Empire planets. However, I told him that I did know the idea was to provoke discontent and, ultimately, rebellion.

The Coordinator smiled. "Well, that's just the starter, Conru. It's a lot more complex than that. Each planet has its own special problems. The Samtraks, for example, had a whole background of cutthroat competition. That was easy: we eliminated that by showing them what *real* cutthroat competition could be like. But Earth is different. Look at it this way. They fight among themselves. Because of their mythical distinctions, not realizing that there are no inferior races, only more or less advanced ones, and that individuals must be judged as individuals, not as members of groups, nations or races. A planet like Earth can be immensely valuable to the Empire, but not if it has to be garrisoned. Its contribution must be voluntary and whole-hearted."

"A difficult problem," I said. "My opinion is that we should treat all exactly alike—*force* them to abandon their unrealistic differences."

"Exactly!" The Coordinator seemed pleased, but, actually, this was pretty elementary stuff. "We're never too rough on the eager lads who come here from Valgol and kick the natives around a bit. We even encourage it when the spirit of rebelliousness dies down."

I told him I had met one.

"Irritating, wasn't it, Conru? Humiliating. Of course, these lads will be reconditioned to civilization when they finish their military service and prepare for more specialized work. Yes, treating all Earthlings alike is the solution. We put restrictions on these colonials; they can't hold top jobs, and so on. And we encourage wild stories about brutality on our part. Not enough to make everybody mad at us, or even a majority—the rumored tyranny has always happened to someone else. But there's a certain class of beings who'll get fighting mad, and that's the class we want."

"The leaders," I chimed in. "The idealists. Brave, intelligent, patriotic. The kind who probably wouldn't be a part of this racial bickering, anyway."

"Right," said the Coordinator. "We'll give them the ammunition for their propaganda. We've *been* doing it. Result: the leaders get mad. Races, religions, nationalities, they hate us worse than they hate each other."

*

The way he painted it, I was hardly needed at all. I told him that.

"Ideally, that would be the situation, Conru. Only it doesn't work that way." He took out a soft cloth and wiped his forehead. "Even the leaders are too involved in this myth of differences and they can't concentrate all their efforts. Luron, of course, would be the other alternative—"

That was a very logical statement, but sometimes logic has a way of making you laugh, and I was laughing now. Luron considered itself our arch-enemy. With a few dozen allies on a path of conquest, Luron thought it could wrest Empire from our hands. Well, we let them play. And each time Luron swooped down on one of the more primitive planets, we let them, for Luron would serve as well as ourselves in goading backward peoples to unite and advance. Perhaps Luron, as a social entity, grew wiser each time. Certainly the primitive colonials did. Luron had started a chain reaction which threatened to overthrow the tyranny of superstition on a hundred planets. Good old Luron, our arch-enemy, would see the light itself some day.

The Coordinator shook his head. "Can't use Luron here. Technologies are entirely too similar. It might shatter both planets, and we wouldn't want that."

"So what do we use?"

"You, Conru. You get in with the revolutionaries, you make sure that they want to fight, you—"

"I see," I told him. "Then I try to stop it at the last minute. Not so soon that the rebellion doesn't help at all—"

The Coordinator put his hand down flat. "Nothing of the sort. They *must* fight. And they must be defeated, again and again, if necessary, until they are ready to succeed. That will be, of course, when they are *totally* against us."

I stood up. "I understand."

He waved me back into the chair. "You'll be lucky to understand it by the time you're finished with this assignment and transferred to another ... that is, if you come out of this one alive."

I smiled a bit sheepishly and told him to go ahead.

"We have some influence in the underground movement, as you might logically expect. The leader is a man we worked very hard to have elected."

"A member of one of the despised races?" I guessed.

"The best we could do at this point was to help elect someone from a minority sub-group of the dominant white race. The leader's name is Levinsohn. He is of the white sub-group known as Jews."

*

"How well is this Levinsohn accepted by the movement?"

"Considerable resistance and hostility," the Coordinator said. "That's to be expected. However, we've made sure that there is no other organization the minority-haters can join, so they have to follow him or quit. He's able, all right; one of the most able men they have, which helps our aims. Even those who discriminate against Jews reluctantly admire him. He's moved the headquarters of the movement out into space, and the man's so brilliant that we don't even know where. We'll find out, mainly through you, I hope, but that isn't the important thing."

"What is?" I asked, baffled.

"To report on the unification of Earth. It's possible that the anarch movement can achieve it under Levinsohn. In that case, we'll make sure they win, or think they win, and will gladly sign a treaty giving Earth equal planetary status in the Empire."

"And if unity hasn't been achieved?"

"We simply crush this rebellion and make them start all over again. They'll have learned some degree of unity from this revolt and so the next one will be more successful." He stood up and I got out of my chair to face him. "That's for the future, though. We'll work out our plans from the results of this campaign."

"But isn't there a lot of danger in the policy of fomenting rebellion against us?" I asked.

He lifted his shoulders. "Evolution is always painful, forced evolution even more so. Yes, there are great dangers, but advance information from you and other agents can reduce the risk. It's a chance we must take, Conru."

"Conrad," I corrected him, smiling. "Plain Mr. Conrad Haugen ... of Earth."

## II

A few days later, I left North America Center, and in spite of the ominous need to hurry, my eastward journey was a ramble. The anarchs would be sure to check my movements as far back as they could, and my story had better ring true. For the present, I must *be* my role, a vagabond.

The city was soon behind me. It was far from other settlement—it is good policy to keep the Centers rather isolated, and we could always contact our garrisons in native towns quickly enough. Before long I was alone in the mountains.

# INSIDE EARTH

I liked that part of the trip. The Rockies are huge and serene, a fresh cold wind blows from their peaks and roars in the pines, brawling rivers foam through their dales and canyons—it is a big landscape, clean and strong and lonely. It speaks with silence.

I hitched a ride for some hundreds of miles with one of the great truck-trains that dominate the western highways. The driver was Earthling, and though he complained much about the Valgolian tyranny he looked well-fed, healthy, secure. I thought of the wars which had been laying the planet waste, the social ruin and economic collapse which the Empire had mended, and wondered if Terra would ever be fit to rule itself.

I came out of the enormous mountainlands into the sage plains of Nevada. For a few days I worked at a native ranch, listening to the talk and keeping my mouth shut. Yes, there was discontent!

"Their taxes are killing me," said the owner. "What the hell incentive do I have to produce if they take it away from me?" I nodded, but thought: *Your kind was paying more taxes in the old days, and had less to show for it. Here you get your money back in public works and universal security. No one on Earth is cold or hungry. Can you only produce for your own private gain, Earthling?*

"The labor draft got my kid the other day," said the foreman. "He'll spend two good years of his life working for them, and prob'ly come back hopheaded about the good o' the Empire."

*There was a time*, I thought, *when millions of Earthlings clamored for work, or spent years fighting their wars, gave their youth to a god of battle who only clamored for more blood. And how can we have a stable society without educating its members to respect it?*

"I *want* another kid," said the female cook. "Two ain't really enough. They're good boys, but I want a girl too. Only the Eridanian law says if I go over my quota, if I have one more, they'll sterilize me! And they'd do it, the meddling devils."

*A billion Earthlings are all the Solar System can hold under decent standards of living without exhausting what natural resources their own culture left us*, I thought. *We aren't ready to permit emigration; our own people must come first. But these beings can live well here. Only now that we've eliminated famine, plague, and war, they'd breed beyond reason, breed till all the old evils came back to throttle them, if we didn't have strict population control.*

\*

"Yeah," said her husband bitterly. "They never even let my cousin have kids. Sterilized him damn near right after he was born."

*Then he's a moron, or carries hemophilia, or has some other hereditary taint*, I thought. *Can't they see we're doing it for their own good? It costs us fantastically in money and trouble, but the goal is a level of health and sanity such as this race never in its history dreamed possible.*

"They're stranglin' faith," muttered someone else.

*Anyone in the Empire may worship as he chooses, but should permission be granted to preach demonstrable falsehoods, archaic superstitions, or antisocial nonsense? The old "free" Earth was not noted for liberalism.*

"We want to be free."

*Free? Free for what? To loose the thousand Earthly races and creeds and nationalisms on each other—and on the Galaxy—to wallow in barbarism and slaughter and misery as before we came? To let our works and culture be thrown in the dust, the labor of a century be demolished, not because it is good or bad but simply because it is Valgolian? Epsilon Eridanian!*

"We'll be free. Not too long to wait, either—"

*That's up to nobody else but you!*

I couldn't get much specific information, but then I hadn't expected to. I collected my pay and drifted on eastward, talking to people of all classes—farmers, mechanics, shopowners, tramps, and such data as I gathered tallied with those of Intelligence.

About twenty-five per cent of the population, in North America at least—it was higher in the Orient and Africa—was satisfied with the Imperium, felt they were better off than they would have been in the old days. "The Eridanians are pretty decent, on the whole. Some of 'em come in here and act nice and human as you please."

Some fifty per cent was vaguely dissatisfied, wanted "freedom" without troubling to define the term, didn't like the taxes or the labor draft or the enforced disarmament or the legal and social superiority of Valgolians or some such thing, had perhaps suffered in the reconquest. But this group constituted no real threat. It would tend to be passive whatever happened. Its greatest contribution would be sporadic rioting.

The remaining twenty-five per cent was bitter, waiting its chance, muttering of a day of revenge—and some portion of this segment was spreading propaganda, secretly manufacturing and distributing weapons, engaging in clandestine military drill, and maintaining contact with the shadowy Legion of Freedom.

Childish, melodramatic name! But it had been well chosen to appeal to a certain type of mind. The real, organized core of the anarch movement was highly efficient. In those months I spent wandering and waiting, its activities mounted almost daily.

*

The illegal radio carried unending programs, propaganda, fabricated stories of Valgolian brutality. I knew from personal experience that some were false, and I knew the whole Imperial system well enough to spot most of the rest at least partly invented. I realized we couldn't trace such a well-organized setup of mobile and coordinated units, and jamming would have been poor tactics, but even so—

*The day is coming.... Earthmen, free men, be ready to throw off your shackles.... Stand by for freedom!*

I stuck to my role. When autumn came, I drifted into one of the native cities, New Chicago, a warren of buildings near the remains of the old settlement, the same gigantic slum that its predecessor had been. I got a room in a cheap hotel and a job in a steel mill.

I was Conrad Haugen, Norwegian-American, assigned to a spaceship by the labor draft and liking it well enough to re-enlist when my term was up. I had wandered through much of the Empire and had had a great deal of contact with Eridanians, but was most emphatically not a Terrie. In fact, I thought it would be well if the redskin yoke could be thrown off, both because of liberty and the good pickings to be had in the Galaxy if the Empire should collapse. I had risen to second mate on an interstellar tramp, but could get no further because of the law that the two highest officers must be Valgolian. That had embittered me and I returned to Earth, foot-loose and looking for trouble.

*

I found it. With officer's training and the strength due to a home planet with a gravity half again that of Earth, I had no difficulty at all becoming a foreman. There was a big fellow named Mike Riley who thought he was entitled to the job. We settled it behind a shed, with the workmen looking on, and I beat him unconscious as fast as possible. The raw, sweating savagery of it made me feel ill inside. *They'd let* this *loose among the stars!*

After that I was one of the boys and Riley was my best friend. We went out together, wenching and drinking, raising hell in the cold dirty canyons of steel and stone which the natives called streets. *Valgolia, Valgolia, the clean bare windswept heights of your mountains, soughing trees and thunderous waters and Maara waiting for me to come home!* Riley often proposed that we find an Eridanian and beat him to death, and I would agree, hiccupping, because I knew they didn't go alone into native quarters any more. I sat in the smoky reek of the bars, half deafened by the clatter and raucousness called music, trying not to think of a certain low-ceilinged, quiet tavern amid the gardens of Kalariho, and sobbed the bitterness of Conrad Haugen into my beer.

"Dirty redskins," I muttered. "Dirty, stinking, bald-headed, sons of bitches. Them and their god-damn Empire. Why, y'know, if 't hadn' been f' their laws I'd be skipper o' my own ship now. I knew more'n that slob o' a captain. But he was born Eridanian—God, to get my hands on his throat!"

Riley nodded. Through the haze of smoke I saw that his eyes were narrowed. He wasn't drunk when he didn't want to be, and at times like this he was suddenly as sober as I was, and that in spite of not having a Valgolian liver.

I bided my time, not too obviously anxious to contact the Legion. I just thought they were swell fellows, the only brave men left in the rotten, stinking Empire; I'd sure be on their side when the day came. I worked in the mill, and when out with the boys lamented the fact that we were really producing for the damned Eridanians, we couldn't even keep the products of our own sweat. I wasn't obtrusive about it, of course. Most of the time we were just boozing. But when the talk came to the Empire, I made it clear just where I stood.

\*

The winter went. I continued the dreary round of days, wondering how long it would take, wondering how much time was left. If the Legion was at all interested, they would be checking my background right now. Let them. There wouldn't be much to check, but what there was had been carefully manufactured by the experts of the Intelligence Service.

Riley came into my room one evening. His face was tight, and he plunged to business. "Con, do you really mean all you've said about the Empire?"

"Why, of course. I—" I glanced out the window, as if expecting to see a spy. If there were any, I knew he would be native. The Empire just doesn't have enough men for a secret police, even if we wanted to indulge in that sort of historically ineffective control.

"You'd like to fight them? Like really to help the Legion of Freedom when they strike?"

"You bet your obscenity life!" I snarled. "When they land on Earth, I'll get a gun somewhere and be right there in the middle of the battle with them!"

18

"Yeah." Riley puffed a cigaret for a while. Then he said, "Look, I can't tell you much. I'm taking a chance just telling you this. It could mean my life if you passed it on to the Eridanians."

"I won't."

His eyes were bleak. "You damn well better not. If you're caught at that—"

He drew a finger sharply across his throat.

"Quit talking like a B-class stereo," I bristled. "If you've got something to tell me, let's have it. Otherwise get out."

"Yeah, sure. We checked up on you, Con, and we think you're as good a prospect as we ever came across. If you want to fight the Eridanians now—*join the Legion* now—here's your chance."

"My God, you know I do! But who—"

"I can't tell you a thing. But if you really want to join, memorize this." Riley gave me a small card on which was written a name and address. "Destroy it, thoroughly. Then quit at the mill and drift to this other place, as if you'd gotten tired of your work and wanted to hit the road again. Take your time, don't make a beeline for it. When you do arrive, they'll take care of you."

I nodded, grimly. "I'll do it, Mike. And thanks!"

"Just my job." He smiled, relaxing, and pulled a flask from his overcoat. "Okay, Con, that's that. We'd better not go out to drink, after this, but nothing's to stop us from getting stinko here."

## III

Spring had come and almost gone when I wandered into the little Maine town which was my destination. It lay out of the way, with forested hills behind it and the sea at its foot. Most of the houses were old, solidly built, almost like parts of the land, and the inhabitants were slow-spoken, steady folk, fishermen and artisans and the like, settled here and at home with the darkling woods and the restless sea and the high windy sky. I walked down a narrow street with a cool salt breeze ruffling my hair and decided that I liked

Portsboro. It reminded me of my own home, twenty light-years away on the wide beaches of Kealvigh.

I made my way to Nat Hawkins' store and asked for work like any drifter. But when we were alone in the back room, I told him, "I'm Conrad Haugen. Mike Riley said you'd be looking for me."

He nodded calmly. "I've been expecting you. You can work here a few days, sleep at my house, and we'll run the tests after dark."

He was old for an Earthling, well over sixty, with white hair and lined leathery face. But his blue eyes were as keen and steady, his gnarled hands as strong and sure as those of any young man. He spoke softly and steadily, around the pipe which rarely left his mouth, and there was a serenity in him which I could hardly associate with anarch fanaticism. But the first night he led me into his cellar, and through a well-hidden trapdoor to a room below, and there he had a complete psychological laboratory.

I gaped at the gleaming apparatus. "How off Earth—"

"It came piece by piece, much of it from Epsilon Eridani itself," he smiled. "There is, after all, no ban on humans owning such material. But to play safe, we spread the purchases over several years, and made them in the names of many people."

"But you—"

"I took a degree in psychiatry once. I can handle this."

He could. He put me through the mill in the next few nights—intelligence tests, psychometry, encephalography, narcosis, psycho-probing, everything his machines and his skill could cover. He did not find out anything we hadn't meant to be found out. The Service had ways of guarding its agents with counter-blocks. But he got a very thorough picture of Conrad Haugen.

In the end he said, still calmly, "This is amazing. You have an IQ well over the borderline of genius, an astonishing variety of assorted knowledge about the Empire and about technical subjects, and an implacable hatred of Eridanian rule—based on personal pique and containing self-seeking elements, but no less firm for that. You're out for yourself, but you'll stand by your comrades and your cause. We'd never hoped for more recruits of your caliber."

"When do I start?" I asked impatiently.

"Easy, easy," he smiled. "There's time. We've waited fifty years; we can wait a while longer." He riffled through the dossier. "Actually, the difficulty is where to assign you. A man who knows astrogation, the use of weapons and machines, and the Empire, who is physically strong as a bull, can lead men, and has a dozen other accomplishments, really seems wasted on any single job. I'm not sure, but I think you'll do best as a roving agent, operating between Main Base and the planets where we have cells, and helping with the work at the base when you're there."

*

My heart fairly leaped into my throat. This was more than I had dared hope for!

"I think," said Nat Hawkins, "you'd better just drop out of sight now. Go to Hood Island and stay there till the spaceship comes next time. You can spend the interval profitably, resting and getting a little fattened up; you look half starved. And Barbara can tell you about the Legion." His leather face smiled itself into a mesh of fine wrinkles. "I think you deserve that, Conrad. And so does Barbara."

Mentally, I shrugged. My stay in New Chicago had pretty well convinced me that all Earthling females were sluts. And what of it?

The following night, Hawkins and I rowed out to Hood Island. It lay about a mile offshore, a wooded, rocky piece of land on which a moon-whitened surf boomed and rattled. The place had belonged to the Hood family since the first settlements here, but Barbara was the last of them.

Hawkins' voice came softly to me above the crash of surf, the surge of waves and windy roar of trees as we neared the dock. "She has more reason than most to hate the Eridanians. The Hoods used to be great people around here. They were just about ruined when the redskins first came a-conquering, space bombardment wiped out their

21

holdings, but they made a new start. Then her grandfather and all his brothers were killed in the revolt. Ten years ago, her father was caught while trying to hijack a jetload of guns, and her mother didn't live long after that. Then her brother was drafted into a road crew and reported killed in an accident. Since then she hasn't lived for much except the Legion."

"I don't blame her," I said. My voice was a little tight, for indeed I didn't. But somebody has to suffer; civilization has a heavy price. I couldn't help adding, "But the Empire's lately begun paying pensions to cases like that."

"I know. She draws hers, too, and uses it for the Legion."

*That, of course, was the reason for the pensions.*

The boat bumped against the dock. Hawkins threw the painter up to the man who suddenly emerged from the shadow. I saw the cold silver moonlight gleam off the rifle in his hand. "You know me, Eb," said Hawkins. "This here's Con Haugen. I slipped you the word about him."

"Glad to know you, Con." Eb's horny palm clasped mine. I liked his looks, as I did those of most of the higher-up Legionnaires. They were altogether different from the low-caste barbarians who were all the rebels I'd seen before. They had a great load of ignorance to drag with them.

We went up a garden path to a rambling stone house. Inside, it was long and low and filled with the memoirs of more gracious days, art and fine furniture, books lining the walls, a fire crackling ruddily in the living room.

"Barbara Hood—Conrad Haugen."

*

Almost, I gaped at her. I had expected some gaunt, dowdy fanatic, a little mad perhaps. But she was—well, she was tall and supple and clad in a long dark-blue evening gown that shimmered against her white skin. She was not conventionally pretty, her face was too strong for all of its fine lines, but she had huge blue eyes and a wide soft mouth and a stubborn chin. The light glowed gold on the hair that tumbled to her shoulders.

I blurted something out and she smiled, with a curious little twist that somehow caught in me, and said merely, "Hello, Conrad."

"Glad to be here," I mumbled.

"The spaceship should arrive in a month or so," she went on. "I'll teach you as much as I can in that time. And you'd better get your own special knowledge onto a record wire, just in case. I understand you've been in the Vegan System, for instance, which nobody else in the Legion knows very much about."

Her tone was cool and business-like, but with an underlying warmth. It was like the sea wind which blew over the islands, and as reviving. I recovered myself and helped mix some drinks. The rest of the evening passed very pleasantly.

Later a servant showed me to my room, a big one overlooking the water. I lay for a while listening to the waves, thinking drowsily how rebellion, when its motives were honest, drew in the best natives of any world, and presently I fell asleep.

The month passed all too quickly and agreeably. I learned things which Intelligence had spent the last three years trying to find out, and dared not attempt to transmit the information. That was maddening, though I knew there was time. But otherwise—

I puttered about the place. There were only three servants, old family retainers who had also joined the anarchs. They had little modern machinery, and of course Earthlings weren't allowed robots, so there was need for an extra man or two. I cut wood and repaired the roof and painted the boathouse, spaded the garden and cleared out brush and set up a new picket fence. It was good to use my hands and muscles again.

And then Barbara was around to help with most of what I did. In jeans and jersey, the sun ablaze on her hair, laughing at my clumsy jokes or frowning over some tough bit of work, she was another being than the cool, lovely woman who talked books and music and history with me in the evenings, or the crisp bitter anarch who spat facts and figures at me like an angry machine. And yet they were all her. I remembered Ydis, who was dead, and the old pain stirred again. But Barbara was alive.

She was more alive to me than most of Valgolia.

I make no apologies for my feelings. I had been away from anything resembling home for some two years now. But I was careful to remain merely friendly with Barbara.

*

She didn't know a great deal about the rebel movement—no one agent on Earth did—but her knowledge was still considerable. There was a fortified base somewhere out in space, built up over a period of four years with the help of certain unnamed elements or planets outside the Empire. I suspected several rival states of that!

Weapons of all kinds were manufactured there in quantities sufficient to arm the million or so rebels of the "regular" force, the twenty million or so in the Solar System and elsewhere who held secret drills and conducted terrorist activities, and the many millions more who were expected to rise spontaneously when the rebel fleet struck.

There was close coordination and a central command at Main Base for the undergrounds of all dissatisfied planets—a new and formidable feature which had not been present in the earlier uprisings. There were rumors of a new and terrible weapon being developed.

In any case, the plan was to assault Epsilon Eridani itself simultaneously with the uprisings in the colonies, so that the Imperial fleet would be recalled to defend the mother world. The anarchs hoped to blast Valgolia to ruin in a few swift blows, and expected that the Empire's jealous neighbors would sweep in to complete the wreckage.

This gentle girl spoke of the smashing of worlds, the blasting of helpless humans, and the destruction of a culture as if it were a matter of insect extermination.

"Have you ever thought," I asked casually once, "that the Juranians and the Slighs and our other hypothetical allies may not respect the integrity of Sol any more than the Eridanians do?"

"We can handle them," she answered confidently. "Oh, it won't be easy, that time of transition. But we'll be free."

"And what then?" I went on. "I don't want to be defeatist, Barbara, but you know as well as I do that the Eridanians didn't conquer all mankind at a single swoop. When they invented the interstellar engine and arrived here, man was tearing the Solar System apart in a war between super-nations that was rapidly reducing him to barbarism. The redskins traded for a while, sold arms, some of their adventurers took sides in the conflict, the government stepped in to protect Eridanian citizens and investments—the side which the Eridanians helped won the war, then found its allies were running things and tried to revolt against the protectorate—and without really meaning to, the strangers were conquering and ruling Earth.

"But the different factions of man still hate each other's guts. There are still capitalists and communists, blacks, whites and Browns, Hindus and Moslems, Germans and Frenchmen, city people and country people—a million petty divisions. There'll be civil war as soon as the Eridanians are gone."

"Some, perhaps," she agreed. "But I think it can be handled. If we have to have civil wars, well, let's get them over with and live as free men."

Personally, I could see nothing in the sort of military dictatorship that would inevitably arise which was preferable to an alien, firm, but just rule that insured stability and a reasonable degree of individual liberty.

But I didn't say that aloud.

*

Another time we talked of the de-industrialization of Earth. Barbara was, of course, venomous about it. "We were rich once," she said. "All Earth was. We have one of the richest planets in the Galaxy.

But because their own world is poor, the redskins have to take the natural resources of their conquests. Earth is a granary and a lumberyard for Valgolia, and the iron of Mars and the petrolite of Venus go back to their industry. What few factories they allow us, they take their fat percentage of the product."

"Certainly they've made us economically dependent," I said, "and their standard of living is undoubtedly higher than ours. But ours has, on the whole, gone up since the conquest. We eat better, we're healthier, we aren't burdened with the cost of past and present and future wars. Our natural resources aren't being squandered. The forests and watersheds and farmlands we ruined are coming back under Eridanian supervision."

She gave me an odd look. "I thought you didn't like the Empire."

"I don't," I growled. "I don't want to be held back just because I'm white-skinned. But I've known enough reddies personally so that I try to be fair."

"It's all right with me," she said. "I can see your point, intellectually, though I can't really *feel* it. But not many of the people will out at Main Base."

"Free men," I muttered sardonically.

We went fishing, and swam in the tumbling surf, and stretched lazily on the beach with the sun pouring over us. Or we might go tramping off into the woods on a picnic, to run laughing back when a sudden rain rushed out of the sky, and afterward sit with beer and cheese sandwiches listening to a wire of Beethoven or Mozart or Tchaikovsky—the old Earthlings could write music, if they did nothing else!—and to the rain shouting on the roof. We might have a little highly illegal target practice, or a game of chess, or long conversations which wandered off every which way. I began to have a sneaking hope that the spaceship would be delayed.

We went out one day in Barbara's little catboat. The waves danced around us, chuckling against the hull, glittering with sunlight, and the sail was like a snow mountain against the sky. For a while we chatted dreamily, ate our lunch, threw the scraps to the hovering gulls. Then Barbara fell silent.

"What's the matter?" I asked.

"Oh, nothing. Touch of *Weltschmerz*, maybe." She smiled at me. "You know, Con, you don't really belong in the Legion."

"How so?" I raised my eyebrows.

"You—well, you're so darned honest, so really decent under that carefully rough surface, so—reasonable. You'll never make a good fanatic."

*Honest!* I looked away from her. The bright day seemed suddenly to darken.

## IV

Spaceships from Main Base had little trouble coming to Earth with their cargoes of guns, propaganda, instructors, and whatever else the rebels on the planet needed. They would take up an orbit just beyond the atmosphere and send boats to the surface after dark. There was little danger of their being detected if they took the usual precautions; a world is simply too big to blockade completely.

Ours dropped on noiseless gravitic beams into the nighted island woods. We had been watching for it the last few days, and now Eb came running to tell us it was here. The pilot followed after him.

"Harry Kane, Conrad Haugen," Barbara introduced us.

I shook hands, sizing him up. He was tall for an Earthling, almost as big as I, dark-haired, with good-looking young features. He wore some approximation of a uniform, dark-blue tunic and breeches, peaked cap, captain's insignia, which gave him a rather dashing look. It shouldn't have made any difference to me, of course, but I didn't like the way he smiled at Barbara.

She explained my presence, and he nodded eagerly. "Glad to have you, Haugen. We need good men, and badly." Then to her: "Get Hawkins. You and he are recalled to Main Base."

"What? But—"

# INSIDE EARTH

A dark exultation lit his face. "The time for action is near—very near! We're pulling all our best agents off the planets. They can work more effectively with the fleet now."

I tried to look as savagely gleeful as they, but inwardly I groaned. How in all the hells was I going to contact Vorka? If I were stranded out in space when the fleet got under way—no, they must have an ultrabeam. I'd manage somehow to call on that even if they caught me at it.

We sent Eb in a boat to get Hawkins while Barbara and I packed a few necessities. Kane paced back and forth, spilling out the news from Main Base, word of mighty forces gathering, rumors of help promised from outside, it was like the thunder which mutters just before a gale.

Presently Hawkins arrived. The old man's calm was undisturbed: he puffed his pipe and said quietly, "I called up my housekeeper, told her my sister in California was suddenly taken sick and I was leaving at once for the transcontinental jetport. Just to account for disappearing, you know. There aren't any Eridanians or Terries hereabouts, but we desperate characters—" he grinned, briefly—"can't be too careful. Brought my equipment along, of course. I suppose they want me to do psychometry on fleet personnel?"

"Something on that order. I don't know."

We made our way through a fine drizzle of rain to the little torpedo of the spaceboat. I looked around into the misty dark and breathed a deep lungful of the cool wet wind. And I saw that Barbara was doing the same.

*

She smiled up at me through the night and the thin sad rain. "Earth is a beautiful world, Con," she whispered. "I wonder if we'll ever see it again."

I squeezed her hand, silently, and we crowded into the boat.

Kane made a smooth takeoff. In minutes we were beyond the atmosphere, Earth was a great glowing shield of cloudy blue behind us, and the stars were bitter bright against darkness. We sent a coded call signal and got a directional beam from the ship. Before long we were approaching it.

I studied the lean black cruiser. She seemed to be of about the same design as the old Solarian interplanetary ships, modified somewhat to accommodate the star drive. Apparently, she was one of those built at Main Base. Her bow guns were dark shadows against the clotted cold silver of the Milky Way. I thought of the death and the ruin which could flame from them, I thought of the hell she and her kind bore—atomic bombs, radiodust bombs, chemical bombs, disease bombs, gravity snatchers, needle beams, disintegrative shells, darkness and doom and the new barbarism—and felt a stiffening within me. Fostering this murderousness was a frightful risk. The main defense against it was Intelligence, and that depended on agents like myself. Perhaps *only* myself.

The crew was rather small, no battles being anticipated. But they were well disciplined, uniformed and trained, a new Solarian army built up from the fragments of the old. The captain was a stiff gray German who had been a leader in the earlier revolt and since fled to space, but most of the officers, such as Kane, were young and violent in their eagerness.

We orbited around the planet for another day or so till all the boats had returned. There was tension in the ship—if the Imperial navy should happen to spot us, we were done. Off duty, we would sit around talking, smoking, playing games with little concentration.

Kane spent most of his free hours with Barbara. They had much to talk about. I swallowed a certain irrational jealousy and wandered around cautiously pumping as many men as I could.

We got under way at last. By this time I had learned that Main Base was a planet, but no more. Only the highest leadership of the Legion knew its location, and they were pledged to swallow the poison they always carried if there seemed to be any danger of capture.

# INSIDE EARTH

For several days by the clocks we ran outward, roughly toward Draco. Our velocity was not revealed, and the slow shift in the outside view didn't help much. I guess that we had come perhaps ten parsecs, but that was only a guess.

*"Approaching Main Base. Stand by."*

\*

When the call rang hollowly down the ship's passageways, I could feel the weariness and tautness easing, I could see homecoming in the faces around me. I stole a glance at Barbara. Her eyes were wide and her lips parted, she looked ahead as if to stare through the metal walls. She had never been here either, here where all her dreams came home.

So we landed, we slipped down out of the dark and the cold and the void, and I heard the rattle and groan of metal easing into place. When the ship's interior grav-field was turned off, I felt a sudden heaviness; this world had almost a quarter again the pull of Earth. But people got used to that quickly enough. It was the landscape which was hard to bear.

They had told us that even though Boreas had a breathable atmosphere and a temperature not always fatally low, it was a bleak place. But to one who had never been far from the lovely lands of Earth, its impact was like a blow in the face. Barbara shuddered close to me as we came out of the airlock, and I put an arm about her waist, knowing the sudden feeling of loneliness which rose in her.

\*

Save for the spaceport and other installations, Main Base was underground. There was no city to relieve the grimness of the scene. We were in a narrow valley between sheer, ragged cliffs that soared crazily into a murky sky. The sun was low, a smouldering disc of dull red like curdling blood; its sullen light glimmered on the undying snow and ice and seemed only to make the land darker. Stars glittered here and there in the dusky heavens, hard and bright and cruel, almost, as in space.

Dark sky, dark land, dark world, with the sheer terrible mountains climbing gauntly for the upper gloom, crags and glaciers like fangs against the dizzy cliffs, with the great shadows marching across the bloody snow toward us, with a crazed wind muttering and whining and chewing at our flesh. It was cold. The cold was like a knife. Pain stung with every breath and eyes watered with tears that froze on suddenly numb cheeks. A great shudder ripped through us and we ran toward the entrance to the city. The snow crunched dry and old under our boots, the cold ate up through the soles, and the wind whistled its scorn.

Even when an elevator had taken us a mile down into the warmth and light of the base, we could not forget. It was a city for a million men and other beings and more than a few women and children, a city of long streets and small neat apartments, hydroponic farms and food synthesizers, schools, shops and amusement places, factories, military barracks and arsenals, even an occasional little flower garden. Its people could live here almost indefinitely, working and waiting for their day of rising.

There was little formality in the civilian areas. Everyone who had come this far was trusted. A man came up to us new arrivals from Earth, asked about conditions there, and then said he would show us to our quarters. Later we would be told to whom we should report for duty.

"Let's go, then, Con," said Barbara, and slipped a cool little hand into mine. I could not refrain from casting a smug backward glance at the somewhat chapfallen Kane.

# V

We slipped quickly into the routine of the place. It was a taut-nerved, hard-working daily round. I could feel the savage expectancy building up like a physical force, but intelligent life is adaptable and we got used to it. There was work to do.

Hawkins was second in command of the psychological service, testing and screening and treating personnel, working on training and indoctrination, and with a voice in the general staff where problems of unit coordination and psychological warfare were concerned. Barbara worked under him, secretary and records keeper and general trouble-shooter. Those were high posts, but both were allowed to retain the nominally civilian status which they preferred.

Their influence and my own test scores got me appointed assistant supervisor of the shipyards. That suited me very well—I was reasonably free from direct orders and discipline, with authority to come and go pretty much as I pleased. They kept me busy; sometimes I worked the clock around, and I did my best to further production of the weapons which might destroy my planet. For whatever I did would make little difference at this late date.

A good deal of my time also went to drill with the armed forces of which, like every able-bodied younger man, I was a reserve member. They put me in an engineer unit and I soon had command of it. I did my best here too, whipping my grim young charges into a sapper group comparable to the Empire's, for I had to be above all suspicion, even of incompetence.

We worked at our learning. We went topside and shivered and manned our guns, set our mines and threw up our bridges, in the racking cold of Boreas. Over ancient snow and ice we trotted, lost in the jumbled wilderness of cruel peaks and railing wind, peeling the skin from our fingers when we touched metal, camped under scornful stars and a lash of drifting ice-dust—but we learned!

My own, more private education went on apace. I found where we were. It was a forgotten red dwarf star out near the shadowy border of the Empire, listed in the catalogues as having one Class III planet of no interest or value. That was a good choice; no spaceship would ever happen into this system by accident or exploration. The anarchs had built their hopes on the one lonely planet, and had named it

Boreas after the god of the north wind in one of their mythologies. My company called it less complimentary things.

The base, including the attached city, was under military command which ultimately led up to the general staff of the Legion. This was a council of officers from half a score of rebellious planets, though Earthlings predominated and, of course, Simon Levinsohn held the supreme authority. I met him a few times, a gaunt, lonely man, enormously able, ridden by his cause as by a nightmare, but not unkindly on a personal level. With just that indomitable heart, the Maccabees had faced Rome's iron legions—Valgolia was greatly interested in the ancient history of a conquered province, knowing how often it held the key to current problems.

There was also a liaison officer from Luron sitting at staff meetings. Luron!

*

When I first saw him, this Colonel Wergil, I stood stiff and cold and felt the bristling along my spine. He looked as humanoid as most of the races at the base. Hairless, faintly scaled greenish-yellow skin, six fingers to a hand, and flat chinless face don't make that breed hideous to me; I have reckoned Ganolons and Mergri among my friends. But Luron—the old and deadly rival, the lesser empire watching its chance to pounce on us, hating us for the check we are on the ambitions of their militarists, Luron.

I have no race prejudices and am willing to take the word of our comparative psychologists that there is no more inherent evil in the Luronians than in any other stock, that the peculiar cold viciousness of their civilization is a matter of unfortunate cultural rather than biological evolution and could be changed in time. But none of this alters the fact that at present they are what they are, brilliant, greedy, heartless, and a menace to the peace of the Galaxy. I have been too long engaged in the struggle between my nation and theirs to think otherwise.

Other states had sent some clandestine help to the Legion, weapons and money and vague promises. Luron, I soon found, had said it would attack us in full strength if the uprising showed a good chance of success, and meanwhile, they gave assistance, credits and materiel and the still more important machine tools, and Wergil's military advice was useful.

I know now, as I suspected even then, that Levinsohn and his associates were not fooled as to Luron's ultimate intentions. Indeed, they planned to make common cause with what remained of Valgolia, as well as certain other traditional foes of their present ally, as soon as they had gained their objectives of independence, and stop any threat of aggression from Luron. It was shrewdly planned, but such a shaky coalition, still bleeding with the hurts and hatreds of a struggle just ended, would be weaker than the Empire, and Luron almost certainly would have sowed further dissension in it and waited for its decay before striking.

The Earthlings have a proverb to the effect that he who sups with the Devil must use a long spoon. But they seemed to have forgotten it now.

The attack, I learned, was scheduled for about four months from the time the agents were recalled. The rebels were counting on the Valgolian power being spread too thinly over the Empire to stand off their massed assault on a few key points. Then, with the home planet a radioactive ruin, with revolt in a score of planetary systems and the ensuing chaos and communications breakdown, and with the Luronians invading, the Imperial fleet and military would have to make terms with the anarchs.

\*

It would work. I knew with a dark chill that it would work. Unless somehow I could get a warning out. That had to be done for more than the protection of Epsilon Eridani, which, even in a surprise attack could defend itself better than these conspirators realized. But all bloodshed should be spared, if possible—and the rebellion did not yet deserve to succeed, for the unity achieved thus far had been the unity of a snake pit against a temporary enemy.

Did it all rest on me? God of space, had the whole burden of history suddenly fallen on *my* shoulders?

I didn't dare think about it. I forced the consequences of failure out of my forebrain, back down into the unconscious, the breeding ground of nightmares, and lived from one day to the next. I worked, and waited, learned what I could and watched for my chance.

But it was not all grimness and concentration. It couldn't be; intelligent life just isn't built that way. We had our social activities, small gatherings or big parties, we relaxed and played. At first I found that gratifying, for it gave me a chance to pump the others. Then I found it maddening, because it kept me from snooping and laying plans. Finally it began to hurt—I was coming to know the anarchs.

They lived and laughed and loved even as humans do. They were basically as decent and reasonable as any similar group of Valgolians. Many were as tormented as I by the thought of the slaughter they readied. There were embittered ones, who had lost all they held dear, and I realized that, while civilization has its price, you can't be objective about it when you are the one who must pay. There were others who had been well off and had chucked all their hopes to join a desperate cause in which they happened to believe. There were children—and what had they done to deserve having their parents gambling away life?

In spite of their appearance, to which I was now accustomed, they were *human*. When I had laughed and talked and sung and drunk beer and danced and arranged entertainments with them, they were my friends.

Moodily, I began to see that I would be one of the price-payers.

I saw most of Hawkins and Barbara, and after them—because of her—Kane. The old psychologist and I got along famously. He would drop into my room for a smoke and a cup of coffee and a drawled conversation whenever he had the chance. His slow gentle voice, his trenchancy, the way the little crinkles appeared around his eyes when he smiled, reminded me of my father. I often wish those two could have met. They would have enjoyed each other.

Then Barbara would stop by on her way from work, or, better yet, she would ask me over to her apartment for a home-cooked dinner. Yes, she could cook too. We would sometimes take long walks down the corridors of the city, we even went up once in a while to the surface for a breath of cold air and loneliness, and it was the most natural thing in the world for us to go hand in hand.

There was no sunlight underground. But when the fluorotube glow shone on her hair, I thought of sunlight on Earth, the high keen light of the Colorado plateaus, the morning light stealing through the trees of Hood Island.

*Ydis, Ydis, I said, once your violet eyes were like the skies over Kalariho, over Kealvigh, our home, pasture land of winds. But it has been so long. It has been ten years since you died—*

I fought. May all the gods bear witness that I fought myself. And I thought I was winning.

# VI

I will never forget one certain evening.

Hawkins and I had come over to Barbara's for supper, and the three of us were sitting now, talking. Wieniawski's Violin Concerto cried its sorrow, muted in the background, and the serene home she had made of the bare little functional apartment folded itself around us. Then Kane dropped in as he often did, with a casualness that fooled nobody, and sat with all his soul in his eyes, looking at Barbara. He was a nice kid. I didn't know why he should annoy me so.

The talk shifted to Valgolia. I found myself taking the side of my race. It wasn't that I hoped to convert anyone, but—well, it was wrong that we should be monsters in the sight of these friends.

"Brutes," said Kane. "Two-legged animals. Damned bald-headed, copper-skinned giants. Wouldn't be quite so bad if they were octopi or insects, but they're just enough different from us to be a caricature. It's obscene."

"Sartons look like a dirty joke on mankind," I said. "Why don't you object to them?"

"They're in the same boat as us."

"Then why mix political and esthetic prejudices? And have you ever thought that you look just as funny to an Eridanian?"

"No race should look odd to another," said Nat Hawkins. He puffed blue clouds. "Even by our standards, the redskins are handsome, in a more spectacular way than humans, maybe."

"And Barbara," I smiled, with a curious little pang inside me, "would look good to any humanoid."

"I should think so," said Kane sulkily. "The redskins took enough of our women."

"Well," I said, "their original conquistadores were young and healthy, very far from home, and had just finished a hard campaign where they lost many friends. At least there were no half-breeds afterward. And since the reconquest none of their soldiers has been permitted to have anything to do with an Earthwoman against her consent. It's not their fault if the consent is forthcoming oftener than you idealists think."

"That sort of thing was more or less standard procedure at home with them, wasn't it?" asked Hawkins.

\*

I nodded. "The harshness of their native world forced them to develop their technology faster than on Earth, so they kept a lot of barbarian customs well into the industrial age. For instance, the rulers of the state that finally conquered all the others and unified the planet took the title *Waelsing*, Emperor, and it's still a monarchy in theory. But a limited monarchy these days, with parliamentary democracy and even local self-government of the town-meeting sort. They're highly civilized now."

"I wouldn't call that spree of conquest they went on exactly civilized."

"Well, just for argument's sake, let's try to look at it from their side," I answered. "Here their explorers arrived at Sol, found a system richer than they could well imagine—and all the wealth being burned up in fratricidal war. Their technical power was sufficiently beyond ours so that any band of adventurers could do pretty much as it wanted in the Solar System, and all native states were begging for their help. It was inevitable that they'd mix in.

"Sure, the Eridanians have been exploiting Solarian resources, though perhaps more wisely than we did. Sure, they garrison unwilling planets. But from their point of view, they're slowly civilizing a race of atomic-powered savages, and taking no more than their just reward for it. Sure, they've done hideous things, or were supposed to have, but there've been plenty of reforms in their policy since our last revolt. They've adopted the—the red man's burden."

"Could be. But Sol wasn't their only conquest."

"Oh, well, of course they had their time of all-out imperialism. There are still plenty of the old school around, starward the course of empire, keep the lesser breeds in their place, and so on. That's one reason why the highest posts are still reserved for members of their own race, another being that even the liberal ones don't trust us that far, yet.

"Their first fifty years or so saw plenty of aggression. But then they stabilized. They had as much as they could manage. To put it baldly, the Empire is glutted. And now, without actually admitting they ever did wrong, they're trying to make up what they did to many of their victims."

"They could do that easily enough. Just let us go free."

\*

"I've already told you why they don't dare. Apart from fearing us, they're economically and militarily dependent on their colonies. You're an American, Nat. Why didn't our nation let the South go its own way when it wanted to secede? Why don't we all go back to Europe and let the Indians have our country?

"And, of course, Epsilon Eridani honestly thinks it has a great civilizing mission, and is much better for the natives than any lesser independence could ever be. In some cases, you've got to admit they're right. Have you ever seen a real simon-pure native king in action? Or read the history of nations like Germany and Russia? And why do we have to segregate races and minorities even in our own organization to prevent clashes?"

"We're getting there," said Nat Hawkins. "It's not easy, but we'll make it."

*Only you're not there yet,* I thought, *and for that reason you must be stopped.*

"You claim they're sated," said Barbara. "But they've kept on conquering here and there, to this very day."

"Believe it or not, but with rare exceptions that's been done reluctantly. Peripheral systems have learned how to build star ships, become nuisances or outright menaces, and the Empire has had to swallow them. Modern technology is simply too deadly for anarchy. A full-scale war can sterilize whole planets. That's another function of empire, so the Eridanians claim—just to keep civilization going till something better can be worked out."

"Such as what?"

"Well, several worlds already have *donagangor* status—self-government under the Emperor, representatives in the Imperial Council, and no restrictions on personal advancement of their citizens. Virtual equality with the Valgolians. And their policy is to grant such status to any colony they think is ready for it."

Hawkins shook his head. "Won't do, Con. It sounds nice, but old Tom Jefferson had the right idea. 'If men must wait in slavery until they are ready for freedom, they will wait long indeed.'"

"Who said we were slaves—" I began.

"You talk like a damned reddie yourself," said Kane. "You seem to think pretty highly of the Empire."

*

I gave him a cold look. "What do you think I'm doing here?" I snapped.

"Yeah. Yeah, sorry. I'm kind of tired. Maybe I'd better go now." Before long Kane made some rather moody good nights and went out.

Nat Hawkins twinkled at me. "I'm a little bushed myself," he said. "Guess I'll hit the bunk too."

When he was gone, I sat smoking and trying to gather up the will to leave. There was a darkness in me. What, after all, *was* I doing here? Gods, I believed I was in the right, but why is right so pitiless?

On Earth they represent the goddess of justice as blind. On Valgolia she has fangs.

Barbara came over and sat on the arm of my chair. "What's the matter, Con?" she asked. "You look pretty grim these days."

"My work's developing some complications," I said tonelessly. My mind added: *It sure is. No way to call headquarters, the rebellion gathering enormous momentum, and on a basis of treachery and racial hatred.*

Barbara's fingers rumpled my hair, the grafted hair which by now felt more a part of me than my own lost crest. "You're an odd fellow," she said quietly. "On the surface so frank and friendly and cheerful, and down underneath you're hiding yourself and your private unhappiness."

"Why," I looked up at her, astonished, "even the psychologists—"

"They're limited, Con. They can measure, but they can't feel. Not the way—"

She stopped, and the light glowed in her hair and her eyes were wide and serious on mine and one small hand stole over to touch my fingers. Blindly, I wrenched my face away.

Her voice was low. "It's some other woman, isn't it?"

"Other—? Well, no. There was one, but she's dead now. She died ten years ago."

*Ydis, Ydis!*

"Your wife?"

I nodded. "We were only married for three years. My daughter is still alive; she's going on twelve now. But I haven't seen her for over two years. She's not on Earth. I wonder if she even thinks of me."

"Con," said Barbara, very softly and gravely, "you can't go on mourning a woman forever."

"I'm not. Forget it. I shouldn't have spoken about it."

"You needed to. That's all right."

"My girl ought to have a mother—" The words came of themselves. What followed thereafter seemed also to happen without my willing it.

Presently Barbara stood back from me. She was laughing, low and sweet and joyous. "Con, you old sourpuss, cheer up! It isn't that bad, you know!"

I managed a wry grin, though it seemed to need all the energies left in me. "You look so happy your fool self that I have to counter-balance it."

"Con, if you knew how I'd been hoping!"

We talked for a long time, but she did most of it—the plans, the hopes, the trip we were going to take and the house we were going to build down by the seashore—"Mary," my daughter, was going to have a home, along with the dozen brothers and sisters she'd have in due course—after the war.

After the war.

I left, finally, stumbling like a blind man toward my quarters. Oh, yes, I loved her and she loved me and we were going to have a home and a sailboat and a dozen children, after the war, when Earth was free. What more could a man ask for?

It had been many years since I'd needed autohypnosis to put myself to sleep, but I used it now.

# INSIDE EARTH

## VII

A month passed.

The delay was partly due to the slowness with which I had to work, even after a plan had been laid. I could only do a little at a time, and the times had to be well separated. Each day brought the moment of onslaught closer, but I dared not hurry myself. If they caught me at my work, there would be an end of all things.

But I cannot swear that my own mind did not prompt me to an unnatural slowness and caution. I was only human, and every day was one more memory.

They had all been very good to us; our friends had a party to celebrate our engagement and we were universally congratulated and all the rest of it. Yes, Kane was there too, shaking my hand and wishing me all the luck in the world. Afterward he went back to his work and his pilot's practice with a strange fierceness.

If at times I fell into glum abstraction, well, I had always been a little moody and Barbara could tease me out of it. Most of the times I was with her, I didn't think about the future at all.

There had been a certain deep inward coldness to her. She had carried the old wound of her losses with bitter dignity. But as the days went on, I saw less and less of it. She would even admit that individual Valgolians might be fine fellows and that the Empire had done a few constructive things for Earth. But it was more than a change of attitude. She was thawing after a long winter, she laughed more, she was wholly human now.

*Human—*

We sat one evening, she and I, in one of the big lounges the base had for its personnel. There were only one or two muted lights in the long quiet room, a breathing of music, snatches of whispering like our own. She sat close against me, and my lips kept straying down to brush her hair and her cheek.

"When we're married—" she said dreamily. Then all at once: "Con, what are we waiting for?"

\*

I looked at her in some surprise.

"Con, why do we assume we can't get married before the war's over?" Her voice was low and hurried, shaking just a little. "The base here has chaplains. It's less than a month now till the business starts. God knows what'll happen then. Either of us might be killed." I heard her gulp. "Con, if they killed you—"

"They won't," I said. "I'm kill-proof."

"No, no. We have so little time, and it may be all we'll ever have. Marry me now, darling, dearest, and at least there'll be something to remember. Whatever comes, we'll have had that while."

"I tell you," I insisted, with a sudden hideous dismay, "there's nothing to worry about. Forget it."

"Oh, I'm not asking for pity. I've more happiness now than is right. Maybe that's why I'm afraid. But, Con, they killed my father and they killed my mother and they killed Jimmy, and if they take you too, it'll be more than I can stand."

The savage woe of an old Earthly poet lanced through my brain:

The time is out of joint     O cursèd spite,     That ever I was born     To set it right!

And then, for just a moment, there came the notion of yielding. *You love the girl, Conru. You love her so much it's a pain in you. Well, take her! Marry her!*

No. I was not excessively tender of heart or conscience, but neither was I that kind of scoundrel.

I kissed her words away. Afterward, alone in the darkness of my room, I realized that Conrad Haugen had no good reason to hang back. It was true, all she said was true, and no other couple was waiting for an uncertain future.

It was the time for action.

\*

I had been ready for days now, postponing the moment. And those days were marching to the time of war, the rebels were quivering to go, a scant few weeks at most lay between me and the ruin of Valgolian plans and work and hope.

In my steadily expanding official capacity, I could go anywhere and do almost anything in an engineering line. So, bit by bit, I had tinkered with the base's general alarm system.

We had scoutships posted, of course, but by the very nature of things they had to be close to the planet or an approaching enemy would slip between them without detection. And the substantial vibrations of a ship traveling faster than light do not arrive much ahead of the ship itself. Whatever warning we had of a hypothetical assault would be very short. It would be signaled to all of us by a siren on the intercommunications system, and after that it would be battle stations, naval units to their ships and all others to such ground defenses as we had.

But modern warfare is all to the offense. There is no way of stopping an attack from space except by meeting it and annihilating it before it gets to its destination. The rebels were counting on that fact to aid them when they struck, but it would, of course, work against them if their enemy should happen to hit first. Everyone was understandably nervous about the chance of our being discovered and assailed.

Working a little at a time, I had put a special switch in the general alarm circuit. It showed up merely as one of many on a sector call board near my room; no one was likely to notice it. And my quarters were not those originally given me. I had moved to a smaller place farther from Barbara, ostensibly to be near my work at the shipyards, actually to be near the base's ultrabeam shack.

Now it was time to act.

I needed an excuse for not going to the gun turret where I was assigned. That involved faking a serious fever, but like all Intelligence men, I had been trained to full psychosomatic integration. The same neural forces that in hysteria produce paralysis, stigmata, and other real symptoms were under my conscious control.

I thought myself sick. By morning I was half delirious and my veins were on fire.

The surgeon general came to see me. "What the hell's the trouble?" he wondered. "This place is supposed to be sterile."

"Maybe it's too damn sterile," I murmured with a perfectly genuine weakness. Then, fighting the light-headedness that hummed and buzzed in me: "*Tsitbu* fever, Doc. I'm sure that's what it is."

"Can't say I've ever heard of it."

"You'll find it in your medical books." He would, too. "It's found on the planet Sirius V, where I once visited. Filter-passing virus, transmitted by airborne spores. Not contagious here. In humans it becomes chronic; no ill effects except a few days' fever like this every few years. Now go 'way and lemme die in peace." I closed my eyes on the distorted and unreal world of sickness.

*

Later Barbara came in, pale and with her hair like a rumpled halo. I had to assure her many times that I was all right and would be on my feet in two or three days. Then she smiled and sat down on the bunk and passed a cool palm over my forehead.

"Poor Con," she said. "Poor squarehead."

"I feel fine as long as you're here," I whispered.

"Don't talk," she said. "Just go to sleep." She kissed me and sat quiet. Hers was the rare gift of being a definite personality even when silent and motionless. I clasped her hand and pretended to fall into uneasy sleep. After a while she kissed me again, very softly, and went out.

I told my body to recover. It took time, hours of time, while the stubborn cells retreated to a normal level of activity. I lay there thinking of many things, most of them unpleasant.

It was well into the night, the logical time to act even if the factories did go on a twenty-four hour basis.

I got up, still swaying a little with weakness, the dregs of the fever ringing in my head. After I had vomited and swallowed a stimulant tablet, I felt better. I put on my uniform, but substituted a plain service jacket without insignia of rank for the tunic. That should make me fairly inconspicuous in the confusion.

Strength came. I glanced cautiously along the dim-lit corridor, and it was empty and silent. I stole out and hurried toward the ultrabeam shack. My hidden switch was on the way; I threw it and ran on with lowered head.

The siren screamed behind me, before me, around me, the howling of all the devils in hell—*Hoo! hoo! Battle stations! Strange ships approaching! Battle stations! All hands to battle stations! Hoo-oo!*

I could imagine the pandemonium that erupted, men boiling out of factories and rooms, cursing and yelling and dashing frantically for their posts—children screaming in terror, women white-faced with sudden numbness—weapons manned, instruments sweeping the skies, spaceships roaring heavenward, incoherent yelling on the intercoms to find out who had given that signal. With luck, I would have fifteen minutes or half an hour of safe insanity.

A few men raced by me, on their way to the nearest missile rack. They paid me no heed, and I hurried along my own path.

The winding stair leading up to the ultrabeam shack loomed before me. I went its length, three steps at a time, bounding and gasping with my haste, up to the transmitter.

It was the tenuous link binding together a score of rebel planets, the only communication with the stars that glittered so coldly overhead. The ultrabeam does not have an infinite velocity, but it does have an unlimited speed, one depending solely on the frequency of the generating equipment, and since it only goes to such receivers as are tuned to its pattern—there must be at least one such tuned unit for the generator to work—it has a virtually infinite range. So men can talk between the stars, but are their words the wiser for that?

\*

Up and up and up, round and round, up and up, metal clanging underfoot and always the demon screech of the siren—up!

I sprang from the head of the stairs and crossed the areaway in one leap to the open door of the shack. There was only one operator on duty, a slim boyish figure before the glittering panel. He didn't hear me as I came behind him. I knocked him out with a calculated blow to the base of the skull. He'd be unconscious for at least fifteen minutes and that was time enough. I heaved his body out of the chair and sat down.

The unit was set for the complicated secret scrambler pattern of the Legion, one which was changed periodically just in case. I twirled the dials, adjusting for the pattern of the set I knew was kept tuned for me at Vorka's headquarters.

The set hummed, warming up. I lifted my eyes and stared into the naked face of Boreas. The shack was above ground, itself dominated by the skeletal tower of the transmitter, and a broad port revealed land and sky.

Overhead the stars were glittering, bright and hard and cruel, flashing and flashing out of the crystal dark. The peaks rose on every side, soaring dizziness of cliffs and ragged snarl of crags, hemming us in with our tiny works and struggles. It was bitterly, ringingly cold out there; the snow screamed when you walked on it; the snapping thunder of frost-split rock woke the dull roar of avalanches, and there was the wind, the old immortal wind, moaning and blowing and wandering under the stars. I saw them running, little antlike men spilling from their nest and racing across the snow before they froze. I saw the ships rise one after the other and rush darkly skyward. The base had come alive and was reaching up to defy the haughty stars.

The set buzzed and whistled, warming up, muttering with the cosmic interference whose source nobody knows. I began to speak into the microphone, softly and urgently: "Calling Intelligence HQ, Sol III, North America Center. Captain Halgan Conru calling North America Center. Come in, Center, come in."

\*

The receiver rustled with the thin dry voice of the stars. Dimly, I could hear the wind outside, snarling around the walls.

"Come in, Center. Come in, Center."

"Captain Halgan!" The voice rattled into the waiting stillness of the shack. "Captain Halgan, is it really you?"

"Get General Vorka at once," I said. "Meanwhile, are you recording? All right, be sure you get this."

I told them everything I knew. I told them what planet this was, and where we were on its surface, and what our strength and plans were. I gave them the disposition of the scoutship pickets, as far as those were known to me, and the standard Legion recognition signals. I finished with an account of the savage differences still existing between Earthman and Earthman, and Earth and its treacherous allies. And all the time I was talking to a recording machine. Nobody was listening.

When I was through, I waited a minute, not feeling any particular emotion. I was too tired. I sat there, listening to the wind and the interstellar whistling, till Vorka spoke to me.

"Halgan! Halgan, you've done it!"

"Shut up," I said. "What's coming now?"

"I checked the Fleet units. We have a Supernova with escort at Bramgar, about fifteen light-years from where you are. You are at their base, aren't you? Can you hold out for two days more?"

"I think so."

"Better get into the hills. We may have to bombard."

"Go to hell." I turned off the set.

Now to get back. They must already know it was a trick; they must be scouring the base for the saboteur. As soon as all loyal men were back, the hunt would really be on.

I had, of course, worn gloves. There would be no fingerprints. And the operator wouldn't know who had attacked him.

I changed the scrambler setting to one picked at random. And in a corner, as if it had fallen there by accident, I dropped a handkerchief stolen from Wergil of Luron. The tiny fragments of tissue which adhere to such a thing could easily be proven to be from him or one of his associates, for the basic Luronian life-molecules are all levo-rotatory. It might help.

I slipped back down the stairs, quickly and quietly. It was over. The base was as good as taken. But there was more to be done. Apart from the saving of my own life, there was still a desperate need for secrecy. For if the rebels knew what was coming, they might choose to stand and fight, or they might flee into the roadless wildernesses of space. Whichever it was, all our work and sacrifice would have gone for little.

*

The provocateur policy is the boldest and most farsighted enterprise ever undertaken. It is the first attempt to make history as we choose, to control the great social forces we are only dimly beginning to understand, so that intelligence may ultimately be its own master.

Sure. Very fine and idealistic, and no doubt fairly true as well. But there is death and treachery in it, loneliness and heartbreak, and the bitterness of the betrayed. Have we the right to set ourselves up as God? Can we really say, in our omniscience, that everyone but us is wrong? There were sane, decent, intelligent folk here on Boreas, the ones we needed so desperately for all civilization. Did we have to make them our enemies, so that their grandchildren might be our friends?

I didn't know. Wherever I turned, there were treason and injustice. However hard I tried to do right, I had to wrong somebody.

I ran on, back to my cabin. I peeled off my clothes and dived into bed, and by the time they looked in on me I had worked back most of my fever.

Don't think, Conru. Don't think of this new victory and the safety of the Empire. And, perhaps, a step closer to the harshly won unity of Earth. Don't think of the way the light catches in Barbara's hair and gets turned into molten gold. You've got a fever to create, man. You've got to think yourself sick again. That ought to be easy.

# VIII

Barbara came in. She was white and still, and presently she leaned her head against my breast and cried quietly, for a long time.

"There is a spy here," she told me.

"I heard about it." I stroked her hair and held her to me, clumsily. "Do you know who it was?"

"I don't know. Somehow, they seem to think the Luronians may be guilty, but they aren't sure. They arrested them, and two were killed resisting. Colonel Wergil is in the brig now, while they decide if Luron can still be trusted."

"It can't," I said. "Earth must win alone."

"We'll win," she said dauntlessly. "With Luron or without it, we'll win." Then, like a little frightened girl, creeping close to me: "But we needed that help so much."

I kissed her and remained silent.

The next day I got on my feet again, weak but recovered. I wandered aimlessly around the base, waiting for Barbara to get through work, listening to people talk. It was ugly, the fear and tension and wolfish watchfulness. *Whom can we trust? Who is the enemy?*

Mostly, they thought the Luronians were guilty. After all, those were the only beings on the planet who had not had to pass a rigorous investigation and psychological examination. But nobody was sure.

Levinsohn spoke over the televisor. His gaunt, lined face had grown very tired, yet there was metal in his voice. The new situation necessitated a change of plans, but the time of assault would, if anything, be moved ahead. "Be of good heart. Stand by your comrades. We'll still be free!"

I went to Barbara's apartment and we sat up very late. But even in this private record I do not wish to say what we talked about.

*

And the next day the Empire came.

There was one Supernova ship with light escort, but that was enough. Such vessels have the mass of a large asteroid, and one of them can sterilize a planet; two or three can take it apart. Theoretically, a task force comprising twenty Nova-class battleships with escorts can reduce one of those monsters if it is willing to lose most of its units. But nothing less can even do significant damage, and the rebel base did not have that much. Nor could they get even what they had into full action.

The ships rushed out of interstellar space, flashing the recognition signals I had given. Before the picket vessels suspected what was wrong, the Valgolians were on them. One managed to bleat a call to base and the alarm screamed again, men rushed to battle stations. Then the Imperials blanketed all communications with a snarl of interference through which nothing the rebels had could drive.

So naturally they were thought to have been annihilated in a few swift blazes of fire and steel, a quick clean death and forgetfulness of defeat. But only the drivers were crippled, and then the Supernova yanked the vessels to its titan flanks and held them in unbreakable gravity beams. The crews would be taken later, with narcotic gas or paralyzer beams—alive.

For the Empire needs its rebels.

I knew the uselessness of going to battle stations, so I hung behind, seeking out Barbara, whose place was with the missile computer bank. I met her and Kane in the hallway. The boy's face was white, and there were tears running down his cheeks.

"This is the end," he said. "They've found us out, and there's nothing left but to die. Good by, Barbara." He kissed her, wildly, and ran for his ship. Moodily, I watched him go. He expected death, and he would get only capture, and afterward—

"What are you doing here, Con?" asked Barbara.

"I'm too shaky to be any good in the artillery. Let me go with you, I can punch a computer."

# INSIDE EARTH

She nodded silently, and we went off together.

*

The floor shook under us, and a crash of rock roared down the halls. The heavy weapons on the Supernova were bloodlessly reducing our ground installations and our ships not yet in action to smashed rubble. They would kill not a single one of us, except by uncontrollable accident, and save many Valgolian and Earth lives that way, but it wasn't pleasant to be slugged. The girl and I staggered ahead. When the lights went out, I stopped and held her.

"It's no use," I said. "They've got us."

"Let me go!" she cried.

I hung on, and suddenly she collapsed against me, crying and shaking. We stood there with the city rumbling and shivering around us, waiting.

Presently the Valgolian commander released the interference and contacted Levinsohn, offering terms of surrender. It seemed to Levinsohn, and it was meant to seem, that further resistance would be useless butchery. His ships were gone and his foes need only bombard him to ruin. He capitulated, and one by one we laid down our arms and filed to meet the victors.

The terms, as announced by messengers—the intercom was out of action—were generous. Leading rebels and those judged potentially "dangerous" would go to penal colonies on various Earthlike planets. Except that they weren't penal colonies at all, but, of course, the Earthlings wouldn't know this. They were indoctrination centers, and, with all my bitterness, I still longed to observe a man like Levinsohn after five years in one of the centers. He'd see things in a different perspective. He'd see the Empire for what it was—even if I sometimes had a little trouble seeing that now—and he'd be a better rebel for it.

Someday Levinsohn and his kind would be back on Earth, the new leaders ready to lead the way to a new tomorrow. And I would be with them.

I'd be back with Levinsohn and the rest, and with Barbara, too, and we'd try to pave the way to the peace and friendship. But meanwhile there'd be other revolutions—striving and hoping and breaking their hearts daring what they thought would be death to win what they called freedom and what we hoped would be evolution.

It was the fire to temper a new civilization.

We walked down the hall, Barbara and I, hand in hand, alone in spite of all the people who were shuffling the same way. Most of them were weeping. But Barbara's head was high now.

"What will happen to us?" she asked.

"I don't know," I said. "But, Barbara, whatever happens after this, remember that I love you. Remember that I'll always love you."

"I love you too," she smiled, and kissed me. "We'll be together, Con. That's all that matters. We'll be together."

That was important—and it made me feel good. Yes, we'd be together; I'd see to that. But for a while Barbara would hate me through all the long years of the indoctrination. Someday, perhaps, she would understand ... the indoctrination could do it, and I could help. But by the gods of space, how would it be to take that hate all that while?

*

We came out into the central chamber where the prisoners were gathering to be herded up to the ships. Armed Valgolian guards stood under the glare of improvised lights. Other Imperials were going through the city, flushing out those who might be hiding and removing whatever our armed forces could use. The equipment would do no one any good here, and Boreas would be left to its darkness.

It was cold in the vast shadowy room. The heating plant had broken down and the ancient cold of Boreas was seeping in. Barbara shivered and I held her close to me. Nat Hawkins moved over to join us, wordlessly.

I was questioned in a locked room by one of the big Valgolian officers. He looked at a stereograph in his hand and he took me aside, but it was not unusual. Many of the starbound prisoners were being questioned by their guards, and I was merely one of them.

"Colonel Halgan?" the officer asked with an eagerness close to hero-worship. He was obviously fresh from school and military terminology came from his lips as if it really meant something to a Valgolian. The colonel, of course, meant that in a titular sense I had been elevated for my work. Funny, if you use the language enough, you get to believe it yourself.

"Sir," the young officer continued, "this is one of the greatest pieces of work I've ever seen. I am to extend the official congratulations of—"

I let him talk for a while and then I raised my hand peremptorily and I told him that the girl with the Earthling Hawkins was to go along for indoctrination, despite the fact that her name did not appear on his lists. He nodded, and I went back to Barbara, but half a dozen men had come between us.

Levinsohn and five guards. The man's carriage was still erect, the old unbreakable pride and courage were still in him. Someone among the prisoners broke loose and rushed at him, cursing, till the Valgolians thrust him back into line.

"Levinsohn!" screamed the man. "Levinsohn, you dirty Jew, you sold us out!"

There you see why this rebellion had to be crushed. Earth still had a long way to go. The Levinsohns, the Barbaras, the more promising of the anarchs would be educated and returned and the civilizing process would go on. Earth's best and bravest would unite and fight us, and with each defeat they would learn something of what we had to teach them, that all races, however divergent, must respect each other and work together, learn it with an intensity which the merely intellectual teaching of schools and propaganda could not achieve alone—or, at any rate, soon enough.

Valgolia is the great and lonely enemy, the self-appointed Devil since none of us can be angels. It is the source of challenge and adversity such as has always driven intelligence onward and upward, in spite of itself.

Sooner or later, generations hence, perhaps, all the subject worlds will have attained internal unity, forgetting their very species in a common bond of intelligence. And on that day Valgolia's work will be done. She and her few friends, her *donagangors*, will seemingly capitulate without a fight and become simply part of a union of free and truly civilized planets.

And such a union will be firmer and more enduring than all the tyrant empires of the past. It will have the strength of a thousand or more races, working together in the harmony which they achieved in struggling against us.

*

That is the goal, but it is a long way ahead; there may be centuries needed, and meanwhile Valgolia is alone.

Barbara would understand. In time she would understand what she as yet did not even know. But first would be the hatred, the cold stark hatred that must come of knowing who and what I really am. I could only wait for that hatred to come after she learned, and then wait for it to go, slowly, slowly....

Lines of the Earthlings were filing forward, and, with Nat Hawkins, Barbara waited for me. I walked to her and took her hand. Her head was high, as high as Levinsohn's. She expected all of us to die, but she'd meet the relatives and friends she thought were dead.

It would be a great, a crushing humiliation, to know one's martyrs were alive and being well treated and intensively educated by the foe, who was supporting and encouraging one's supposedly dangerous revolution.

"It won't be so bad as long as we're together, darling," I said.

She smiled, misunderstanding, and kissed me defiantly before our Valgolian guards.

www.ingramcontent.com/pod-product-compliance
Lightning Source LLC
Chambersburg PA
CBHW050907120626
46554CB00003B/1060